Written by Johannah Gilman Paiva
Illustrated by Lauren Pashuk

In a book full of color, on a wonderful day,
Lyla and Jack wake up ready to play!
They explore all the colors, starting with red.
They put on red shoes and socks
as they jump out of bed!

"We should dress as white ghosts,"
Jack says to his bear.

Then a funny white bunny
appears from nowhere.

Lyla sees yellow flowers
and a yellow pear tree,

Jack sees a yellow duck
and a striped yellow bee.

Jack picks orange pumpkins
that he wants to buy.

Lyla bought orange carrots
to give them a try.

Lyla has a green turtle
who she likes to walk.

Jack sees a green frog
who thinks he can talk.

Lyla picks purple flowers,
while watching for bees.

Jack eats purple plums,
while sitting in trees.

Lyla sees a brown robin
catch a worm for her nest.

Jack and his brown dog
like brown ice cream the best.

Lyla dreams of pink birds
each rehearsing their parts,
While wearing pink glasses
that are shaped like pink hearts.

Jack ties on blue sneakers
because laces are cool.

Lyla rides her blue bike
past her pretty blue pool.

Gray Cat chases Gray Mouse,
which they both think is fun.

Then gray clouds fill the sky,
and they block out the sun.

The gray clouds bring rain showers
that start from a mist.
Then build up to a pour,
and this day takes a twist.

Like a thief in the night,
rain steals colors away,
Draining every last drop
from this colorful day.

With the color all gone,
the sky turns to **black**.

Lyla knows he is scared,
so she holds hands with Jack.

Then, when they get home,
Jack falls flat on his face,
spilling lots of bright colors
all over the place.

There's red, and there's blue,
and there's pink, and there's green.
Jack has found every color
that he's ever seen!

Now there's a rainbow of color
everywhere that they look,
And that's why Jack and Lyla
love to play in this book!

You may lose your colors
on a gray, rainy day,
But color is too wonderful
to be taken away.

So there's no need to worry
when the sky turns to black.
The sun always comes out
and color always comes back!